I Like to Read® books, created by award-winning
picture book artists as well as talented newcomers,
instill confidence and the joy of reading in new readers.

We want to hear every new reader say, "I like to read!"

_____

Visit our website for flash cards, activities, and more about the series:
www.holidayhouse.com/ILiketoRead
#ILTR
This book has been tested by an educational expert
and determined to be a guided reading level G.

To my family,
who has always pushed me toward my dreams,
inspired me, and supported me every step of this journey.
Konnorónhkwa

Arihhonni, pronounced AH-lee-HOO-nee, means "He is the charge"
in the Kanien'keha (Mohawk) language, spoken by members of the Akwesasne community.
Also known as Honni (HOO-nee), he is a member of the Haudenosaunee people.

Haudenosaunee (HOH-deh-noh-SHOH-nee): People of the Longhouse
Kanien'keha (g'NYEN-geh-HAH): Mohawk
Kanienkehaka (g'NYEN-geh-HAH-gah): Mohawk people
Konnorónhkwa (GOHN-uh-LOON-gwah): I love you.
Niawen (NYAH-wahn): Thank you.
Tota (DEW-dah): Elder

I LIKE TO READ is a registered trademark of Holiday House Publishing, Inc.
Text and illustrations copyright © 2023 by Cannon David
All Rights Reserved
HOLIDAY HOUSE is registered in the U.S. Patent and Trademark Office.
Printed and bound in December 2022 at C&C Offset, Shenzhen, China.
The artwork was created with digital tools.
www.holidayhouse.com
First Edition
1 3 5 7 9 10 8 6 4 2

Library of Congress Cataloging-in-Publication Data

Names: David, Arihhonni, author, illustrator.
Title: Who will win? / Arihhonni David.
Description: First edition. | New York : Holiday House, [2022] | Series: I like to read
Audience: Ages 4-8. | Audience: Grades K-1. | Summary:
"When a quick-footed bear and a quick-witted turtle race across a frozen
lake, Turtle has a secret plan to win!"—Provided by publisher.
Identifiers: LCCN 2021042652 | ISBN 9780823449484 (hardcover)
Subjects: CYAC: Bears—Fiction. | Turtles—Fiction. | Racing—Fiction.
LCGFT: Picture books.
Classification: LCC PZ7.1.D3359 Wh 2022 | DDC [E]—dc23
LC record available at https://lccn.loc.gov/2021042652

ISBN: 978-0-8234-4948-4 (hardcover)

# Who Will Win?

## Arihhonni David

I Like to Read®

HOLIDAY HOUSE • NEW YORK

Bear has fast legs.
Turtle has a fast mind.
Who will win the race?

Turtle will go under the ice.

Bear will go over the ice.

Ready.

Set.

**GO!**

Bear runs fast.

# "Here I am!"

Turtle says.

Bear runs faster.

Where is Turtle now?

Bear runs even faster!

Where is Turtle now?

Turtle wins the race!

How did he do it?

Turtle's family helped him.

"Here we are!"

Turtle calls to Bear,
"Come back!"

Turtle and Bear

share the prize.

Bear has fast legs.
Turtle has a fast mind—
and a big family.